Pig Jumps Over the Moon

by Jeff Dinardo - illustrated by Dave Clegg

RED
CHAIR
·PRESS·

Everyday, without fail,
Cow jumped over the moon.

"Amazing!" said the Cat with the fiddle.
"She is terrific!" said the Dish and the Spoon.

Pig saw it too.
"I wish I could do that," he said.

When he thought no one was looking,
Pig jumped in the air.

He didn't get very far.

"You are not in shape," said Humpty.
"You have to exercise," said Miss Muffet.

The next day Pig got up early.
He ran two times around the yard.

He jumped rope while he worked.
He even started to eat fruits and vegetables.

One day Pig knew he was ready.
He took a running start and jumped
as high as he could.

Up, up he went.
Over roof tops and tree tops.
Pig kept going up!

Finally he soared over the moon.
Even the man in the moon smiled.

"I made it!" said Pig.
"But, hey, it's a long way down!"

"Hop on" said a voice.
It was Cow.

Then Pig and Cow landed safely back
on the ground. Everyone cheered.
Pig had done it.

Big Question: What was Pig's big goal? What did Pig do when he wanted to get in shape?

Big Words:

exercise: activity done to improve health and fitness

soared: fly or rise high in the air

vegetable: a plant or part of a plant used as food